To all essential workers—
past, present, and future—
with respect and admiration

Essential es·sen·tial \
i-ˈsen(t)-shəl adj.
absolutely necessary;
of the greatest importance

ATHENEUM BOOKS FOR YOUNG READERS

An imprint of Simon & Schuster Children's Publishing Division
1230 Avenue of the Americas, New York, New York 10020
© 2023 by Lulu Delacre. Book design by Lissi Erwin © 2023 by
Simon & Schuster, Inc. Photos on p. 30-31 © iStock/Getty Images.
All rights reserved, including the right of reproduction in whole or
in part in any form.

ATHENEUM BOOKS FOR YOUNG READERS is a registered trademark
of Simon & Schuster, Inc. Atheneum logo is a trademark of
Simon & Schuster, Inc. For information about special discounts for
bulk purchases, please contact Simon & Schuster Special Sales at
1-866-506-1949 or business@simonandschuster.com.
The Simon & Schuster Speakers Bureau can bring authors to your
live event. For more information or to book an event, contact the
Simon & Schuster Speakers Bureau at 1-866-248-3049 or visit our
website at www.simonspeakers.com.
The text for this book was set in Maduki Regular, Causten Round,
Crayon Crumble, Kidprint MT Pro Bold and .Kopik Regular.
The illustrations for this book were rendered in collage.
Manufactured in China
0523 SCP
First Edition
10 9 8 7 6 5 4 3 2 1

Library of Congress Cataloging-in-Publication Data
Names: Delacre, Lulu, author, illustrator.
Title: Veo, veo, I see you / Lulu Delacre.
Description: First edition. | New York : Atheneum Books for Young
Readers, [2023] | Includes author's note. | Audience: Ages 4-8. |
Audience: Grades K-1. | Summary: "While out
running errands with their mami during the Covid-19
pandemic, Marisol and Pepito play a game of Veo, Veo (I Spy) that
helps them see how the workers in their neighborhood are, and
will always be, essential"—Provided by publisher.
Identifiers: LCCN 2022007024 (print) | LCCN 2022007025 (ebook)
| ISBN 9781665911917 (hardcover) | ISBN 9781665911924 (ebook)
Subjects: CYAC: Occupations—Fiction. | COVID-19
Pandemic, 2020—Fiction. | Hispanic Americans—Fiction.
Classification: LCC PZ7.D3696 Ve 2023 (print) | LCC PZ7.D3696
(ebook) | DDC [E]—dc23
LC record available at https://lccn.loc.gov/2022007024
LC ebook record available at https://lccn.loc.gov/2022007025

VEO, VEO, I SEE YOU

Lulu Delacre

atheneum

Atheneum Books for Young Readers
New York London Toronto Sydney New Delhi

Mami is the best cook
at Rosita's Café!
... Was.

The restaurant closed.

A bad virus—
too easy to catch
in small, crowded places—
was going around.

The smell of onions and peppers fried in garlicky oil wafts through the house.

I gaze out the window
as Mami packs
her arroz con pollo
for Cousin Johnny and
Tía Olga's almuerzo,
and . . .
I know just the game
for Pepito, Mami, and
me to play!

Veo, veo . . .
¿Qué ves?
I see the bus driver!
Conductor de bus.
Muy necesario.
To get to Tía Olga's!
Essential.

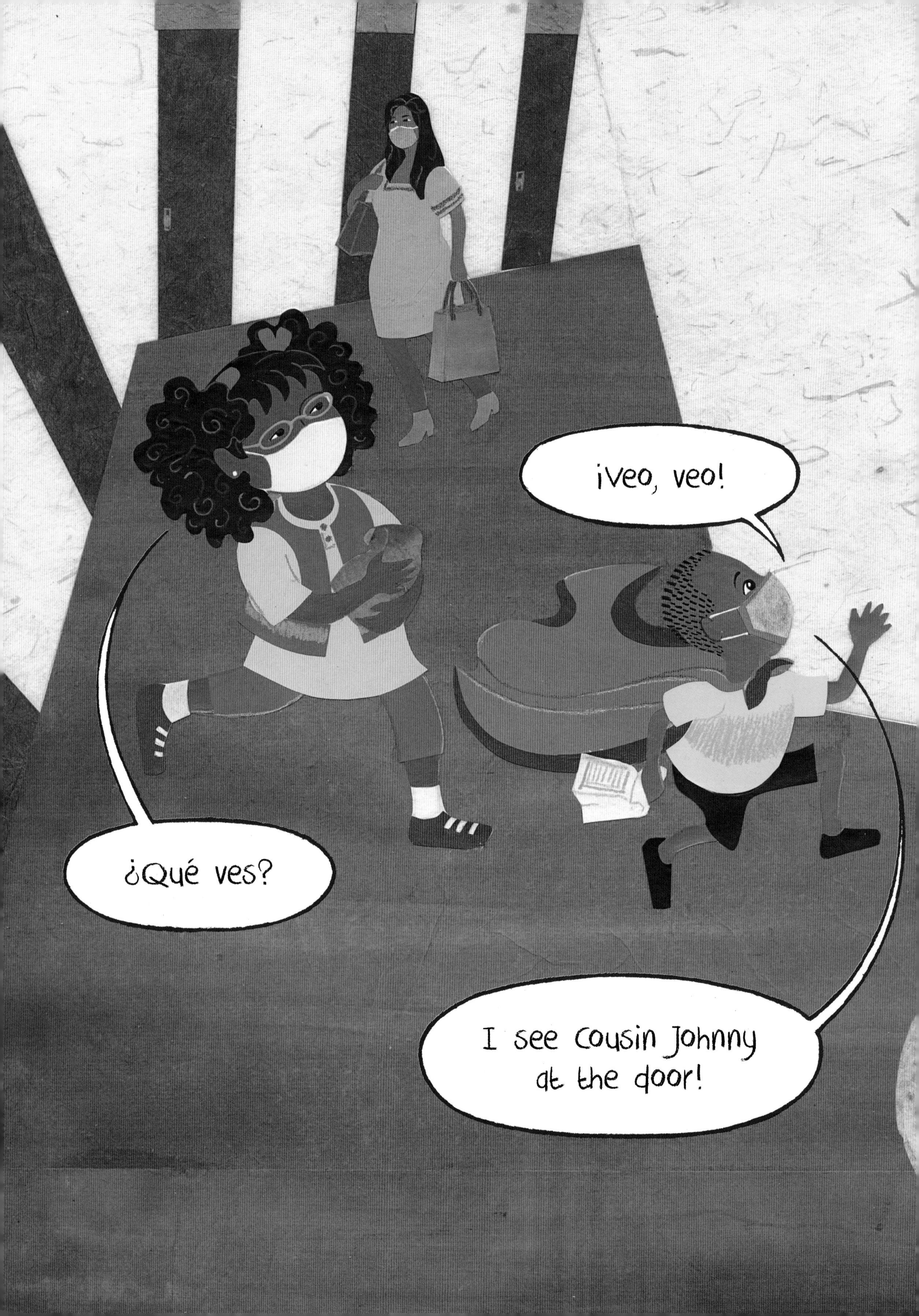
¿Qué ves?
¡Veo, veo!
I see Cousin Johnny at the door!

Pepito hands Tía Olga's
medicine
to Cousin Johnny.
Tía Olga shrieks and claps
at the aroma
of Mami's arroz con pollo.

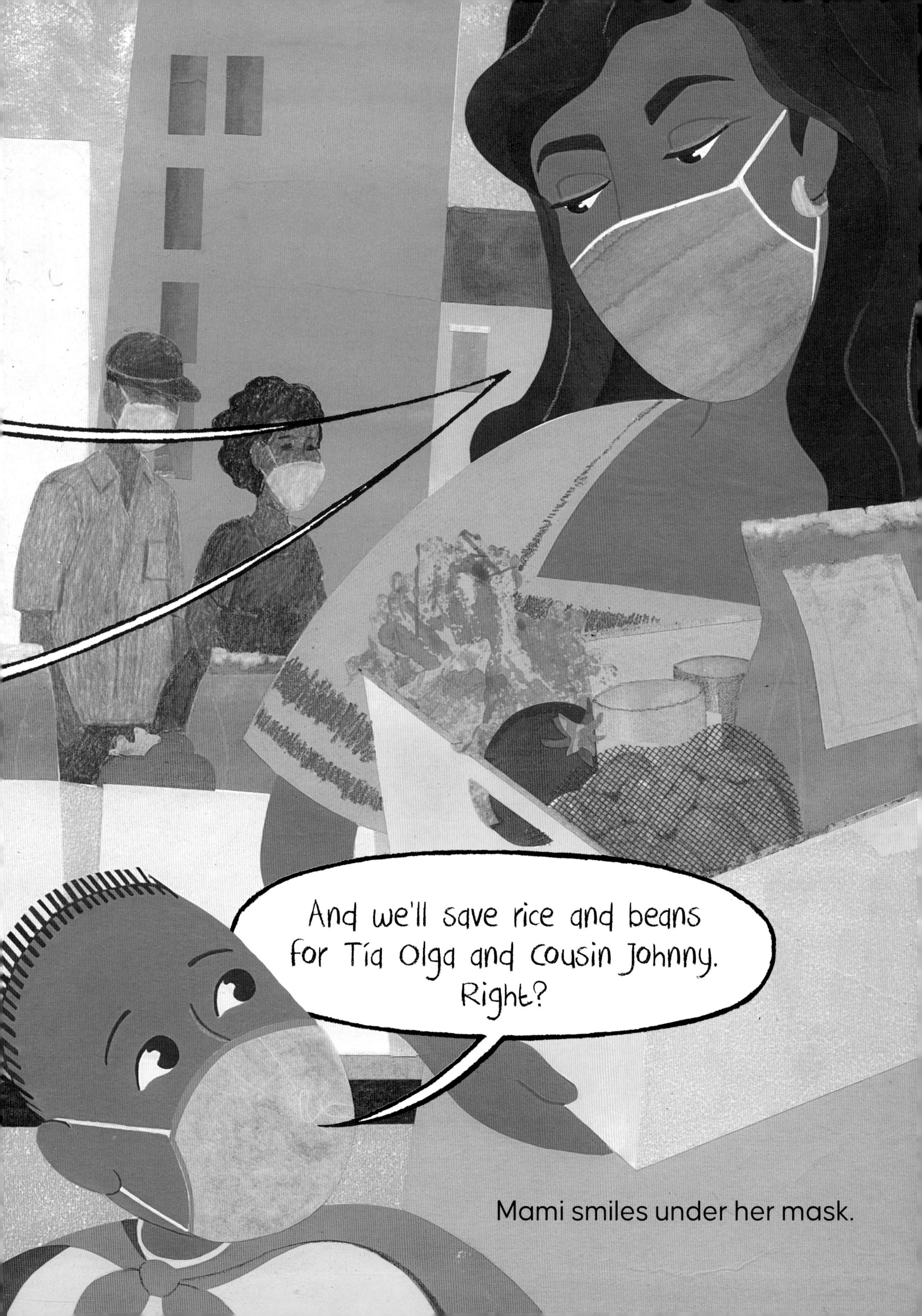

Mami smiles under her mask.

Back at the house,
we play no more.
Now I see
what I had not before.
What can I do
to show what I know
is true?

I have an idea!

Pepito helps me.
He finds pretty pictures
in old magazines,
which I cut out
for all to see.

When I'm done,
we hold Mami by the hands
and together go outside
to wonder at the windows.

People stop and stare,
surprised by my sign.

Neighbors call neighbors.

People come out.
Workers see that we see them.
And lifted by that,
they give it up for each other.
Claps and cheers
ripple far out.

Author's Note

The year 2020 brought a worldwide pandemic. To protect people from getting sick, many local governments throughout the United States ordered everyone to stay home for many months.

Workers who state governments agreed were **essential** were exempt from the stay-at-home orders. They were needed to keep the country going. They could not work from home to avoid catching the deadly virus.

Essential workers included people in the healthcare field, like nurses and doctors, and those in food production, like Marisol's neighbors at the chicken plant and the food pantry. But many other people were needed for all our neighborhoods to function. Trash collectors, bus drivers, pharmacists, cashiers, electricians, plumbers, landscapers, firefighters, and police officers all kept going to work. Essential workers, who according to government statistics were disproportionately Black and Brown, risked their lives daily to protect their communities—to protect all of us. They worked in jobs that allowed the rest of us to go about our daily lives and meet our basic needs.

Before the pandemic, many of us did not think about how important these workers were for our society to function properly. They were invisible.

Not anymore.

"What is essential is invisible to the eye."
—Antoine de Saint-Exupéry,
The Little Prince

farm

fishery

grocery

fire station

pharmacy

hardware store

police station